Stories of Magical Animals

Retold by
Carol Watson

Adapted by Gill Harvey

Illustrated by Nick Price

Reading Consultant: Alison Kelly
University of Surrey Roehampton

Chapter 1

Pegasus

Long ago in Greece, there lived a handsome prince named Bellerophon*. He was strong, brave, and loved by everyone... except the king.

3

* say bel-**lair**-o-fon

The king wanted to get rid of Bellerophon. So, he thought up a plan and sent for the prince.

"Think you're brave, do you?" he sneered. "We'll soon see about that."

You must kill the Chimera*, a terrible beast that keeps eating my people.

4

Eager to obey his king, Bellerophon set off to find the monster. On the way, an old lady stopped him.

"First, you must catch the winged horse, Pegasus," she said.

"Find Pegasus and you will be safe from the beast. Pegasus is strong and swift and flies like a bird."

After searching for days,
Bellerophon found the horse
high up in the mountains.
"What a beauty," he gasped.

Pegasus was wild and free,
with powerful beating wings.
Catching him wouldn't be easy.

In a flash of silvery light,
the goddess Athene* appeared.
She held out a golden bridle
to Bellerophon.

This is a magic bridle. It will help you catch Pegasus.

"If you put this over the horse's head, Pegasus will become tame," she said.

7

Bellerophon thanked Athene and hid behind a rock near a river. When Pegasus came to drink, Bellerophon tiptoed out.

Very quietly, he crept up to Pegasus and slipped the bridle over the horse's head.

Startled, Pegasus reared up.

"Steady," said Bellerophon.
The horse calmed down and
Bellerophon climbed onto
his back.

Spreading his wings, Pegasus
soared into the sky.

9

As they flew on, the air grew hot, steamy and smelly.

"Ugh!" said the prince as he sniffed. "That's disgusting! We must be near the Chimera."

They flew down in time to see the beast leaving its cave.

The Chimera didn't have just one head. It had two: a goat-head, with terrible horns, and a  lion-head which breathed fire.

Even its tail was an evil-looking snake. It spat at Bellerophon, trying to sting him with poison.

Pegasus flew closer and the prince fired his arrows. The lion roared. Huge flames shot from its mouth.

Pegasus rose above the fire and Bellerophon shot more arrows. They struck the goat-head and the snake-tail.

Then the prince took out his spear and stuck a lump of lead on the end of it.

The mouth of the lion-head opened wide to roar and Bellerophon plunged his spear down the lion-head's throat.

As the lead melted, the lion-head gave a howl of pain and the beast collapsed. The Chimera was dead.

Bellerophon went back to the king and told him the good news.

I've killed the Chimera, your majesty!

The king wasn't too pleased, but his people were delighted.

"Bellerophon's a hero," they cried. "He's like a god!"

All this praise made
Bellerophon big-headed.

"Maybe I
am a god,"
he said. "If
I beat the
Chimera, I
must be!"
So he flew
to Mount
Olympus,
where the
gods lived.

Time to
go home.

Zeus, the king of the gods, was annoyed to see the prince and sent a bee to sting Pegasus. The horse reared up, throwing Bellerophon off.

Bellerophon fell through the clouds to the ground and was killed in an instant.

Then Zeus caught Pegasus and rode him home to Mount Olympus.

Faster, Pegasus, faster!

From that day on, Pegasus lived with the gods, pulling Zeus across the sky in a chariot made of gold.

Chapter 2

The greedy griffin

Hassan was a farmer, but the only animals on his farm were his two beloved oxen.

One day, he was working in the fields when, suddenly, the sky went dark.

Hassan looked up. Was it about to rain? But he didn't see a cloud overhead...

...he saw a griffin! A griffin was a terrifying creature. It had the head and wings of an eagle, but the body of a lion.

Swooping down, the griffin snatched up the two oxen in its lion's claws.

Hassan ran away in terror. With a few flaps of its giant wings, the griffin was gone.

Back at home, Hassan sat down and wept.

"There is no hope," he sobbed. "The griffin will eat my oxen. I have nothing." His friends tried to cheer him up.

We'll go and rescue them!

Feeling a little better, Hassan and his friends set off to find the griffin. For hours they climbed, higher and higher into the mountains.

All at once, Hassan stopped.

Higher up the mountain still, they came across what they thought was a strange plant.

"What a funny tree," said one of the men.

Hassan shook his head. "It's not a tree," he said.

It's a griffin's feather!

24

Just then, they heard a loud noise. *Ahhhhhhh... uhhhhh.*

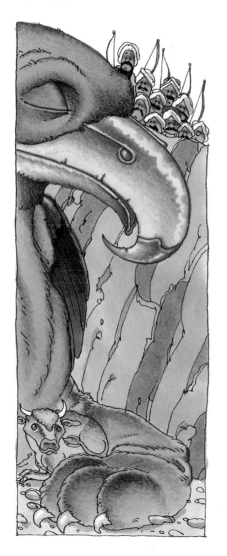

"W-w-w-what's that?" the men whispered, looking over the rocks.

There was the griffin, fast asleep and snoring, with the ox trapped by its paw.

"Quick, before it wakes!" cried Hassan. As fast as they could, the men put arrows to their bows and fired them.

The griffin woke up with a mighty bellow. But it was too late.

A hail of arrows struck its chest. As the griffin fell back, Hassan's ox jumped up and ran to safety.

And, from then on, whenever Hassan worked in his fields, he checked for strange clouds first.

Chapter 3

The evil cockatrice

There was once a farmer named Zak. He and his wife, Beela, were happy but very poor. Their only animals were a few hens and a rooster.

One day, the rooster began
running around and around in
circles, while
crowing
loudly.

"Beela!
Come and
look at this!"
called Zak.

Cock-a-
doodle-
doo!

The rooster sat down and ruffled its feathers.

"He looks like he's about to lay an egg," said Beela.

"But roosters can't!" said Zak.

They stared. This one *had* laid an egg and it was huge.

30

A few minutes later, the
egg began to crack. A tiny
rooster
comb
appeared.

The rooster stared at the
egg with its
beady eyes.
Suddenly it
gave a great
squawk and
rolled over,
dead.

Zak and Beela gasped in
horror as a snake crawled out
of the egg. It sat up proudly
and looked around.

Beela saw its beady red eyes
and pointy rooster's comb.

"A cockatrice!" she
screamed.

"What's a cockatrice?" asked Zak.

"It's a very evil creature," said Beela. "It's only born when a rooster lays an egg."

The cockatrice slithered off. Everything it touched was burned, leaving a horrible scorched trail.

Anything that looked into the creature's creepy red eyes died immediately.

"We must warn everyone!" cried Beela. She and Zak ran to the village leader.

The cockatrice is dangerous!

The village leader sent a brave soldier to kill the cockatrice. The soldier wore a helmet to protect his eyes and blindfolded his horse, too.

"Do be careful!" Beela called out, as he left.

The soldier rode along, looking for the cockatrice.

When he found a scorched field, he knew it was near. Then he saw it.

Charging up, he raised his spear and stabbed the cockatrice as hard as he could.

As the spear went in, the soldier shouted out in pain. It was as though poison had shot up the spear into his arm.

My arm! It's burning!

He fell from his horse and lay still, unable to move. The cockatrice wasn't hurt at all.

37

The villagers were terrified that the cockatrice would kill them all.

"Perhaps the old priest can help," said Zak.

Let's see... You'll need a mirror.

"To kill the creature, you must show it a reflection of itself," the priest said.

Zak and Beela ran off to
fetch the biggest mirror they
could find. Then they hid
behind some rocks, to wait.

When the cockatrice arrived,
they crept forward, holding
the mirror in front of them.

As soon as the cockatrice saw itself, it let out a desperate shriek.

Zak and Beela peeked around the mirror. The cockatrice was dead on the ground. Its evil eyes had claimed their last victim.

Chapter 4

Unicorn magic

Once, there was a king who believed unicorn horns were magic. "Find me a unicorn!" he cried to Toby, his page. "And don't come home without one."

41

Toby hunted all over the world, but he couldn't find a unicorn anywhere.

The king is crazy! I don't believe unicorns exist.

Days became weeks... weeks became months... months became years...

Toby grew old, but he didn't dare go home empty-handed. He had just one place left to try – the mountains of Tibet.

There, he met an old man whose granddaughter knew where a unicorn lived.

For days they journeyed.
Toby's feet hurt and his bones
ached.

Finally, the girl said, "The
unicorn lives around this bend.
But if I show you, you must
promise to leave him alone."

Toby didn't say anything.
There, in front of them, was
a unicorn. At last, he could
go home.

But Toby went home alone.
Even if the king was angry,
he couldn't touch the
unicorn.

When Toby told
the king, he was
shaking with fear.
"Oh well,"
said the king.
"If I can't have
a real unicorn,
I'll put them on my banner."
"You might have thought of
that before!" said Toby, but he
said it to himself.

Try these other books in
Series One:

Animal Legends: The secrets of the animal kingdom revealed. Find out why cats hate rats, why monkeys live in trees and how rabbits took their revenge on a grumpy crocodile.

Dragons: Stan must outwit a dragon to feed his children and Victor must persuade two dragons not to eat him.

The Burglar's Breakfast: Alfie Briggs is a burglar, who discovers someone has stolen his breakfast!

The Dinosaurs Next Door: Mr. Puff's house is full of amazing things. Best of all are the dinosaur eggs – until they begin to hatch...

Series editor: Lesley Sims

Designed by
Katarina Dragoslavic

This edition first published in 2007 by Usborne Publishing Ltd.,
Usborne House, 83-85 Saffron Hill, London EC1N 8RT, England.
www.usborne.com
Copyright © 2007, 2003, 1982 Usborne Publishing Ltd.